# Dear Parents:

Congratulations! Your child is taking the first steps on an exciting journey. The destination? Independent reading!

**STEP INTO READING**® will help your child get there. The program offers five steps to reading success. Each step includes fun stories and colorful art or photographs. In addition to original fiction and books with favorite characters, there are Step into Reading Non-Fiction Readers, Phonics Readers and Boxed Sets, Sticker Readers, and Comic Readers—a complete literacy program with something to interest every child.

## Learning to Read, Step by Step!

**Ready to Read   Preschool–Kindergarten**
• big type and easy words • rhyme and rhythm • picture clues
For children who know the alphabet and are eager to begin reading.

**Reading with Help   Preschool–Grade 1**
• basic vocabulary • short sentences • simple stories
For children who recognize familiar words and sound out new words with help.

**Reading on Your Own   Grades 1–3**
• engaging characters • easy-to-follow plots • popular topics
For children who are ready to read on their own.

**Reading Paragraphs   Grades 2–3**
• challenging vocabulary • short paragraphs • exciting stories
For newly independent readers who read simple sentences with confidence.

**Ready for Chapters   Grades 2–4**
• chapters • longer paragraphs • full-color art
For children who want to take the plunge into chapter books but still like colorful pictures.

**STEP INTO READING**® is designed to give every child a successful reading experience. The grade levels are only guides; children will progress through the steps at their own speed, developing confidence in their reading.

Remember, a lifetime love of reading starts with a single step!

Special thanks to Venetia Davie, Ryan Ferguson, Sarah Lazar, Charnita Belcher, Tanya Mann, Julia Phelps, Nicole Corse, Sharon Woloszyk, Rita Lichtwardt, Carla Alford, Rob Hudnut, David Wiebe, Shelley Dvi-Vardhana, Gabrielle Miles, Julie Osborn, Rainmaker Entertainment, and Patricia Atchison and Zeke Norton

Published in the United States by Random House Children's Books, a division of Random House LLC, 1745 Broadway, New York, NY 10019, and in Canada by Random House of Canada Limited, Toronto, Penguin Random House Companies.

Visit us on the Web!
StepIntoReading.com
randomhousekids.com

Educators and librarians, for a variety of teaching tools, visit us at RHTeachersLibrarians.com

ISBN 978-0-553-50890-1 (trade) — ISBN 978-0-375-97415-1 (lib. bdg.) — ISBN 978-0-553-50891-8 (ebook)

Printed in the United States of America

10 9 8 7 6 5 4 3 2 1

Barbie in Princess POWER

SAVING THE DAY!

Adapted by Melissa Lagonegro

Based on the screenplay by Marsha Griffin

Illustrated by Ulkutay Design Group

Random House 🏠 New York

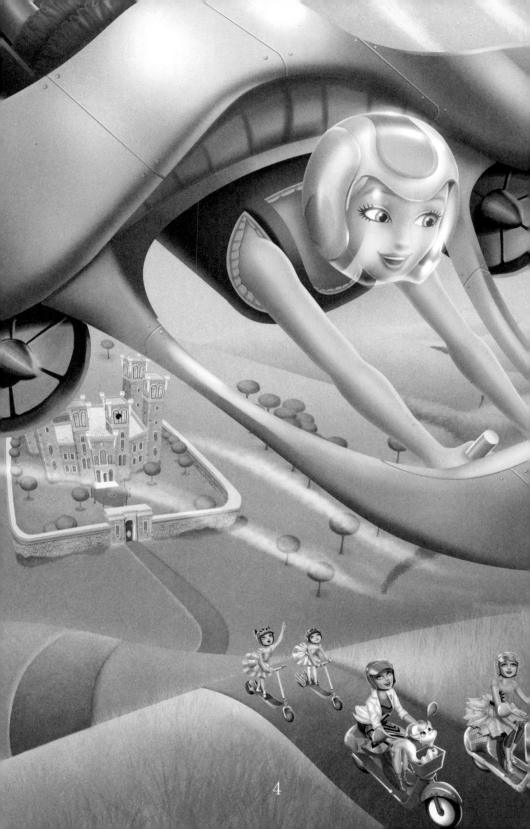

Princess Kara loves
to go on adventures.
She flies in a machine
made by her friends,
Makalya and Madison.

Kara crashes into a tree.

She is not hurt.

The king and queen
are mad.

They want Kara
to stay out of danger.

Baron Von Ravendale
is the king's advisor.
He makes a magic potion.
He will use it to take over
the kingdom!

The potion spills!

It falls onto a caterpillar.

The caterpillar turns

into a sparkly butterfly!

The friends have tea.
Kara's jealous cousin,
Corinne, joins them.

The sparkly butterfly
flies around Kara.
It kisses her.

The butterfly gives Kara
special powers!
"You are a superhero!"
says Madison.

Kara's friends make
her a costume.
Now Kara is
Super Sparkle!

The city is in trouble.

Super Sparkle flies

to the rescue.

Everyone in the city
loves Super Sparkle!
Kara loves
being a superhero!

Corinne learns that Kara
is Super Sparkle.
She wants superpowers,
too!
Corinne finds the
magic butterfly.

She becomes
Dark Sparkle!
She wants to be better
than Super Sparkle.

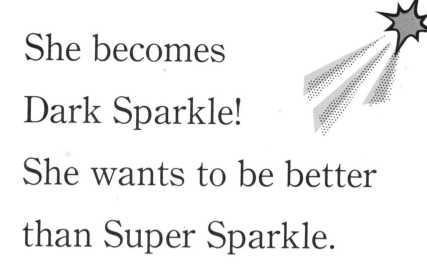

Everyone finds out that
Kara is Super Sparkle.
The king and queen are
very angry with her.
She put herself in danger!

The baron drinks
a new potion.
He gets superpowers!
Now he can take over
the kingdom!

The baron attacks
the royal family.
Kara and Corinne turn
into Super Sparkle
and Dark Sparkle.
The girls argue over
who should fight him.

Super Sparkle and
Dark Sparkle need
to work as a team
to stop the baron.

Super Sparkle
and Dark Sparkle
defeat him together!

Everyone is safe,
thanks to Kara
and Corinne.

They will keep working
together to make the
kingdom a better place.